Ma Sally was the best cook in Charleston County, South Carolina. Everybody knew it, especially Ma Sally. When she fixed supper, the tables groaned under crocks of collard greens, piles of sweet potatoes, and heaps of hot rolls. But Ma Sally was most famous for her black-eyed peas. When she brought them to the Sunday evening potluck at First Baptist, folks lined up just to get a taste.

Ma Sally had a son, John, who was the kindest, most thoughtful man you could hope to meet. When John passed the corner restaurant on his way home after coaching the neighborhood baseball team, Miss Harriet would run out to meet him with something from the kitchen. On Sundays, Miss Hannah sat in the front row of the church choir so she could see John in the first pew. And Miss Hattie, the town librarian, made sure that John's book requests were always ready for him.

One morning John sat down to a huge breakfast Ma Sally had cooked for him—grits with melted cheese, sizzling bacon, eggs over easy, and a stack of pancakes you almost couldn't see over.

"Ma," said John, "I think I'd like to get married."

Ma Sally frowned. "I ain't sure about these local gals, John. I don't think they'd feed you right. Have you tried Miss Harriet's cornbread? Dry as dust and sour as three-week-old milk."

John nodded thoughtfully, then said, "True, don't no one around here seem to be able to cook like you. But I have to make my own way in life. I think I'd like to get married just the same."

Ma Sally was troubled. She figured it was time for John to raise a family of his own, but she couldn't bear the thought of her only child sitting down to an ill-cooked meal. "Anybody who wants to marry my John," she thought, "will have to cook as well as me."

The next time Ma Sally went into town, she mentioned to Ma'am Della, the town grocer and a known gossip, that John was lookin' to get hitched. Any interested ladies, she whispered, should come to her house that Sunday evening.

When Pastor Vernon stopped by the grocery for green tomatoes, Ma'am Della told him. Harriet, shopping nearby, heard.

Reginald shouted to Mr. Mosely over the noise of his barber's clippers that John was going to choose a bride that Sunday evening. And Hannah, hidden under the hair dryers, heard.

First-grader Flannery told her brother that there would be a contest to pick the best lady in town for John. And Hattie, shelving books nearby, heard.

And on Saturday afternoon, ancient Mr. Jefferson told even-more-ancient Ms. Grady the news. And the new girl in town, fresh out of college and sharp as a tack, well, she heard, too.

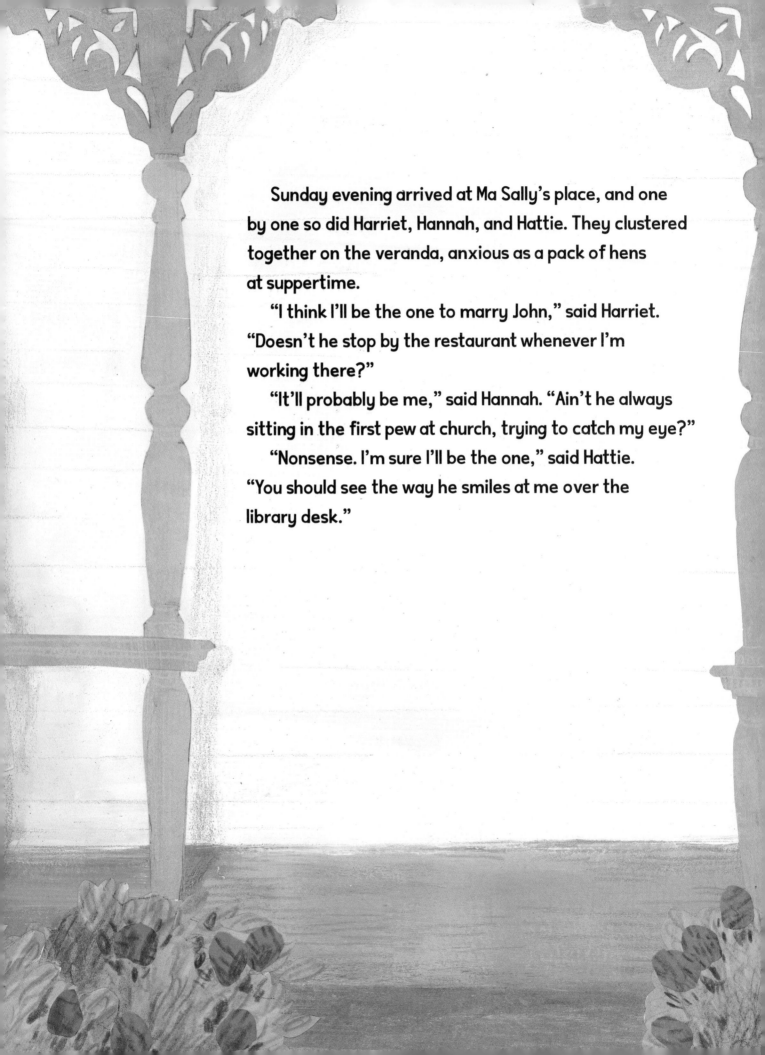

Sunday evening arrived at Ma Sally's place, and one by one so did Harriet, Hannah, and Hattie. They clustered together on the veranda, anxious as a pack of hens at suppertime.

"I think I'll be the one to marry John," said Harriet. "Doesn't he stop by the restaurant whenever I'm working there?"

"It'll probably be me," said Hannah. "Ain't he always sitting in the first pew at church, trying to catch my eye?"

"Nonsense. I'm sure I'll be the one," said Hattie. "You should see the way he smiles at me over the library desk."

A mighty fight was brewin' on the front porch when Ma Sally flung open the door. "Come in," she said. She led them into the kitchen.

"Ladies," said Ma Sally, "if you want a chance at John, you're going to need to cook."

"Cook!" whined Harriet.

"Cook?" shrieked Hannah.

"Cook?!" shouted Hattie.

"Cook," said Ma Sally. "And not just anything. Y'all are going to cook up a dish of black-eyed peas. Whoever makes the best peas marries my son. It's as simple as that."

And so they cooked. They made a terrible mess. At last, three bowls of black-eyed peas sat on the kitchen table.

Slowly, Ma Sally tasted each one. She chewed thoughtfully. She swallowed.

Harriet's peas were too mushy.

Hannah's peas were too salty.

Hattie's peas tasted like nothing at all.

Ma Sally shook her head. "I'm sorry, ladies. I'm afraid not a one of y'all is fit for my son."

Harriet pouted. Hannah sulked. Hattie frowned.

Suddenly there was a knock at the door.

A voice called, "May I come in?"

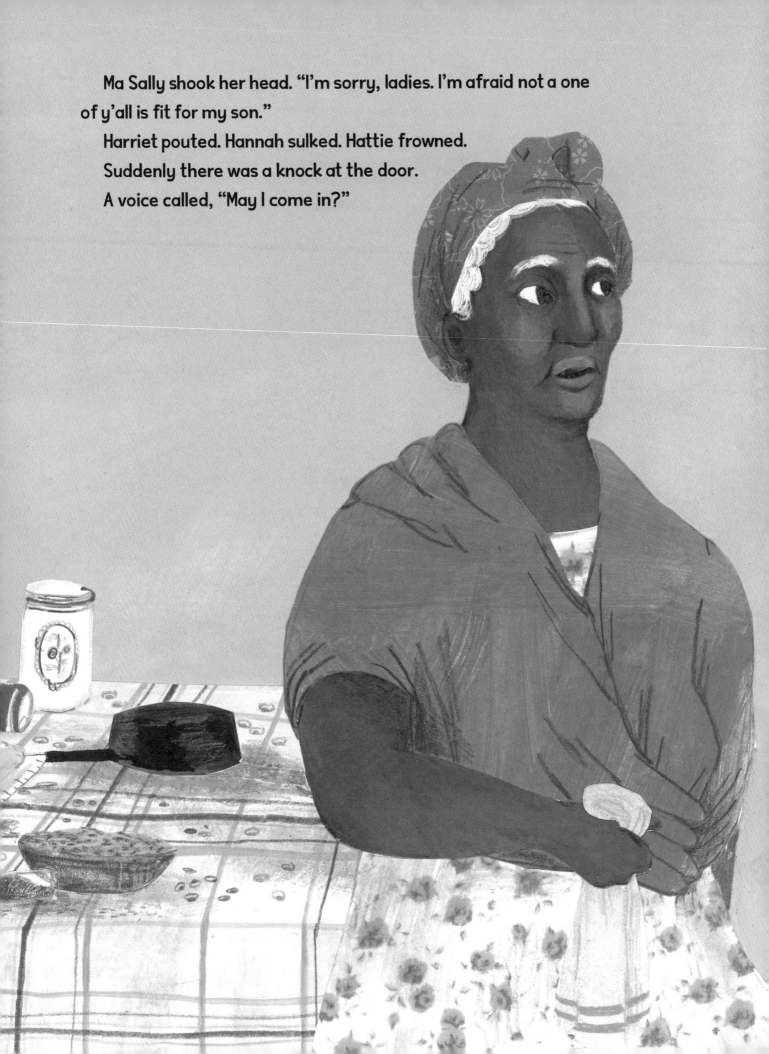

In walked a capable-looking young lady. "I heard there was some kind of contest happenin' here," she said in a voice as sweet as molasses. "May I try?"

"Who," snapped Hattie, "are you?"

"My name," said the girl, "is Princess."

"Princess?" asked Hannah. "What sort of name is that?"

"It's the name my pa and ma gave me," said the girl simply, "because I'm special."

"If you're so special," said Ma Sally, "prove it. Cook them peas."

Everyone crowded around the stove to watch, but Princess paid them no mind. She cooked like she was born to do it. She whirled about the kitchen, slicing, dicing, and stirring. Ingredients flew into the pot one after another, until the peas were simmering away. A delicious smell filled the room. Finally, sweeping the lid off the pot, Princess announced simply, "Peas are done."

Ma Sally dipped a spoon into the pot and took a bite. "These peas," she whispered. Everyone held their breath. "These peas are the best I've ever tasted!"

John let out a whoop and a holler.

Princess smiled. "Thank you," she said. "My momma taught me to cook peas like this, and her momma taught her."

"Well," said Ma Sally, "maybe you can teach my John." She hugged Princess so tight it's a wonder the girl didn't get bruised all over.

"How about it?" Ma Sally asked. "You and John are two peas in a pod."

Princess frowned. "Hmmm . . . I don't know. I like John well enough, but I've got my own plans. How about this—dancing Saturday at the juke joint?" John nodded, his mouth too full to speak.

Princess continued, "And one more thing. I know I'm the best cook there is, but what can you do, John?" She looked around the kitchen. "Why don't you show me how you scrub them pots and pans?"

In the blink of an eye, John was up to his elbows in dishwater. When he finished, John looked at Princess questioningly, and she smiled and nodded. Ma Sally, brushing aside tears of joy, turned to get herself more of those peas. But by that time they were all gone.

And come next spring . . .

Author's Note

Growing up, I was always confused by the classic fairy tale "The Princess and the Pea." Why was it so important that the princess be sensitive enough to feel a pea through all those mattresses? Who could possibly be that delicate, anyway? I decided to rewrite this story to be about the things I think are truly important—love and family. In particular, I wanted to represent an African-American community full of vibrant individuals, each of whom has something unique to bring to the table. I imagined this story, set in the mid-1950s, taking place among the first stirrings of the civil rights movement, when it became more important than ever for African Americans—particularly in the South—to maintain strong, close-knit communities.

Princess's Black-Eyed Peas

Not too spicy, but with enough flavor to make you come back for seconds. Serves four.

Be sure to get a grown-up's help to make this recipe.

Ingredients:

8 oz. dry black-eyed peas
4 slices bacon or 4 T. butter
½ onion, chopped
1 stalk celery, chopped
1 T. garlic powder
1 t. paprika
Salt and black pepper, to taste

Place peas in a large pot and add 3 ½ cups of water. Bring to a boil, and simmer for two minutes. Remove from heat and allow peas to soak, covered, for one hour. Do not drain the water.

If using bacon, cook it in a large skillet until crispy. Remove bacon and reserve for topping. If using butter, melt it over medium heat. Add onion and celery to bacon drippings or melted butter and cook until tender. Add garlic powder, paprika, salt, and pepper, and stir well.

Add mixture to peas and return to heat. Simmer, covered, over medium heat for about 35 minutes or until peas are tender, stirring occasionally. Crumble the reserved bacon, if prepared, on top of peas as they are served.

Enjoy!

To black families everywhere

Published by Charlesbridge, 85 Main Street, Watertown, MA 02472
(617) 926-0329 · www.charlesbridge.com

Library of Congress Cataloging-in-Publication Data
Name: Himes, Rachel, author, illustrator.
Title: Princess and the peas / Rachel Himes.
Description: Watertown, MA : Charlesbridge, [2017] | Summary: In this version of the classic story, Ma Sally of Charleston County,
South Carolina, devises a contest for her son's admirers: cook up a dish of black-eyed peas that meets her exacting standards,
and the winner can marry her son. Includes recipe for Princess's black-eyed peas.
Identifiers: LCCN 2016013779 (print) | LCCN 2016031874 (ebook) | ISBN 9781580897181 (reinforced for library use) |
ISBN 9781607348849 (ebook) | ISBN 9781607348856 (ebook pdf)
Subjects: LCSH: African Americans—South Carolina—Charleston County—Juvenile fiction. | Cooking (Peas)—Juvenile fiction. |
Contests—Juvenile fiction. | Mothers and sons—Juvenile fiction. | Mothers-in-law and daughters-in-law—Juvenile fiction. |
Charleston County (S.C.)—Juvenile fiction. | CYAC: African Americans—Fiction. | Cooking (Peas)—Fiction. | Contests—Fiction. |
Mothers and sons—Fiction. | Courtship—Fiction. | Charleston County (S.C.)—Fiction.
Classification: LCC PZ7.1.H567 Pr 2017 (print) | LCC PZ7.1.H567 (ebook) | DDC 813.6 [E]—dc23
LC record available at https://lccn.loc.gov/2016013779

Printed in China
(hc) 10 9 8 7 6 5 4 3 2 1

Illustrations done in acrylic, watercolor, ink, pencils, and collage on Arches paper
Display type set in Billy Serif by SparkyType
Text type set in Helenita by RodrigoTypo
Color separations by Colourscan Print Co Pte Ltd, Singapore
Printed by 1010 Printing International Limited in Huizhou, Guangdong, China
Production supervision by Brian G. Walker
Designed by Susan Mallory Sherman